Ladybird  Readers

In a Plane

Based on the Peppa Pig
TV series

Picture words

Peppa

George

Mommy
Pig

Daddy
Pig

Captain
Dog

Wendy
Wolf

Danny
Dog

Pedro
Pony

Ladybird Readers

In a Plane

Text adapted by Sorrel Pitts
Series Editor: Sorrel Pitts

LADYBIRD BOOKS

UK | USA | Canada | Ireland | Australia
India | New Zealand | South Africa

Ladybird Books is part of the Penguin Random House group of companies
whose addresses can be found at global.penguinrandomhouse.com.
www.penguin.co.uk   www.puffin.co.uk   www.ladybird.co.uk

Text adapted from 'Peppa Pig: Peppa Goes Around the World', first published 2016
This version published by Ladybird Books 2018
001

This book is based on the
TV Series 'Peppa Pig'.
'Peppa Pig' is created by
Neville Astley and Mark Baker.
Peppa Pig © Astley Baker Davies Ltd/
Entertainment One UK Ltd 2003.

www.peppapig.com

Printed in China

A CIP catalogue record for this book is available from the British Library

ISBN: 978–0–241–31945–1

All correspondence to:
Ladybird Books
Penguin Random House Children's
80 Strand, London WC2R 0RL

MIX
Paper from
responsible sources
FSC® C018179

mountains

jungle

South Pole

desert

lizard

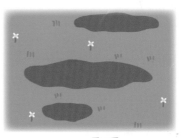

muddy puddles

Suzy Sheep

Emily Elephant

Edmond Elephant

"It's the holidays!"
said Wendy Wolf.

"I want to jump in muddy puddles," said Peppa.

"My holiday is in the jungle," said Pedro Pony.

"Ours is in the desert," said Emily and Edmond Elephant.

"Mine is in the
mountains!"
said Danny Dog.

"Mine is at the
South Pole," said
Suzy Sheep.

Peppa and George
got into the car.

"Let's go to the
park," said Peppa.
"I want to jump in
muddy puddles!"

Daddy Pig started driving.
Then, Peppa and George
heard . . .

Bang!

Clang!

Bonk!

The car stopped.

"Oh no," said Daddy Pig.

"We need help,"
said Mommy Pig.

"Look!" said Peppa.
"Miss Rabbit is here!"

"Don't worry," said Miss Rabbit. "You can fly to the park!"

The family flew in
Miss Rabbit's plane.

"That isn't a park,"
said Daddy Pig.
"It's a jungle!"

Peppa smiled. Pedro was on holiday in the jungle!

The plane flew down.

Bump!

"Hello, Pedro!" said Peppa.

"Hello, Peppa!" said Pedro.
"It's great in the jungle."

The jungle was fun, but
there were no puddles.

"Let's go to the mountains!"
said Peppa.

Shooooom!

Danny Dog loved
the mountains.

"It's quiet here,"
said Captain Dog.

Whhhiirrrr!

The plane stopped in front of Danny and Captain Dog!

"Hello, Danny!" said Peppa. "We're flying to lots of great places!"

19

Soon, the plane flew
to a desert.

"Emily and Edmond
are there!" said Peppa.

The plane stopped
in the desert.

"Hello, Emily!
Hello, Edmond!"
said Peppa.

"We saw a lizard, but it ran from us," said Edmond.

"Oh no!" said Mommy Pig.

"There's the lizard!"
said Daddy Pig.

"Let's go to the
South Pole!" said Peppa.
"Suzy is there."

Squeak!

Suzy loved the South Pole, but she wanted to see Peppa.

Skiiiiddd!
Screech!

Peppa's plane stopped
on the snow.

Suzy was very happy
to see her friend!

Peppa had fun at the South Pole, but there were no puddles!

"Our car must be OK now," said Mommy Pig.

The plane flew into the sky.

Whooosh!

W hooosh!

"Hello!" said Miss Rabbit. "You can drive your car now."

"Flying in a plane was nice," said Peppa, "but there weren't any . . ."

"... muddy puddles!"
Peppa and her family
loved muddy puddles!

Activities

The key below describes the skills
practiced in each activity.

Spelling and writing

Reading

Speaking

? Critical thinking

Preparation for the Cambridge
Young Learners exams

1 Wendy Wolf   **a**

2 Pedro Pony   **b**

3 Danny Dog   **c**

4 Suzy Sheep   **d**

2 Find the words.

holiday
mountain
jungle
puddle
lizard

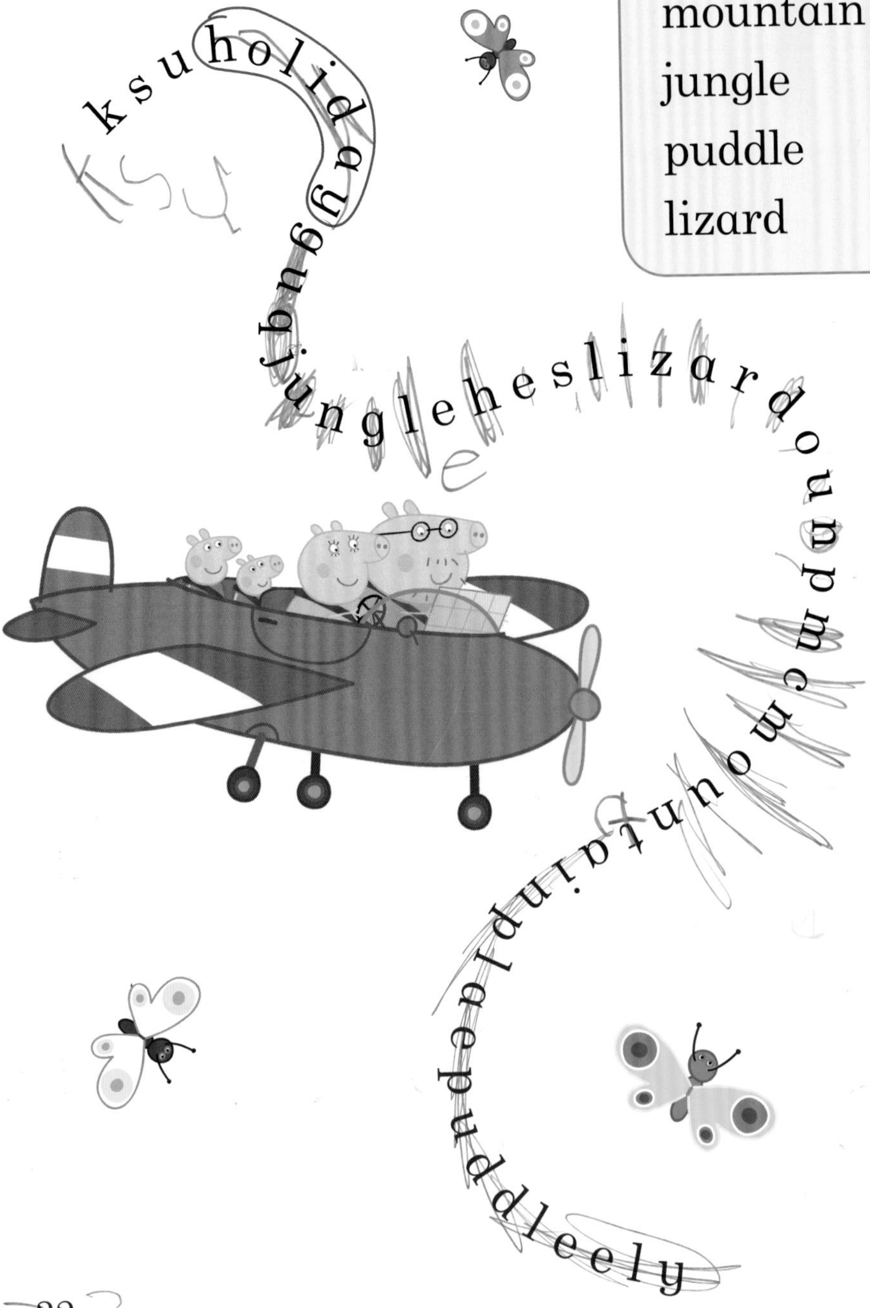

ksuholiday

jungleheslizard

mountain

puddle

3 Look and read. Put a ☑ or a ☒ in the boxes. 📖 ⬡

1 This is Peppa. ✓

2 This is Daddy Pig. ☐

3 This is Wendy Wolf. ☐

4 This is Captain Dog. ☐

5 This is the jungle. ☐

 **4** **Look and read. Write *yes* or *no*.**

"It's the holidays!" said Wendy Wolf.

"I want to jump in muddy puddles," said Peppa.

1 Peppa is with her friends.   yes

2 Peppa and her friends are at the South Pole.

3 Peppa wants to swim in the sea.

4 Peppa wants to jump in the mountains.

5 Peppa wants to jump in muddy puddles.

5 Who said this? 📖 ✏️ ⬡

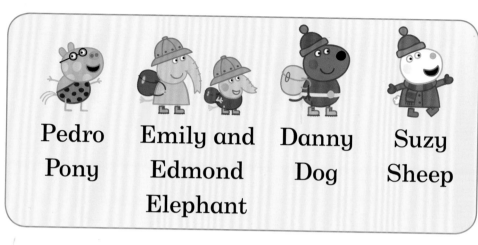

Pedro Pony   Emily and Edmond Elephant   Danny Dog   Suzy Sheep

1 "My holiday is in the jungle,"

said _Pedro Pony_ .

2 "Mine is at the South Pole,"

said _Es Mang_ .

3 "Mine is in the mountains!"

said _____ .

4 "Ours is in the desert,"

said _____

_____ .

6 Talk to a friend about holidays. 💬 ❓

"My holiday is in the jungle," said Pedro Pony.

"Mine is in the mountains!" said Danny Dog.

"Ours is in the desert," said Emily and Edmond Elephant.

"Mine is at the South Pole," said Suzy Sheep.

1 *Where's your favorite holiday?*

My favorite holiday is in the mountains.

2 Would you like to go to the desert?

3 Would you like to go to the jungle?

4 Would you like to jump in muddy puddles? Why? / Why not?

7 Circle the correct sentences.

1
a Peppa and Pedro got into the car.
b Peppa and George got into the car.

2
a "Let's go to the puddle," said Peppa.
b "Let's go to the park," said Peppa.

3
a "I want to jump in muddy puddles!" said Peppa.
b "I want to jump in muddy mountains!" said Peppa.

4
a Peppa and George heard . . . Bang! Clang! Bonk!
b Mommy Pig said, "Bang! Clang! Bonk!"

8 Look, match, and write the words.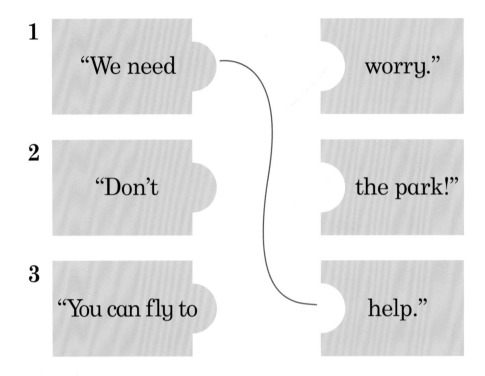

1   "We need   worry."

2   "Don't   the park!"

3   "You can fly to   help."

1 "We need help." ....

2 ....

3 ....

9 **Circle the correct words.**

1 Miss Rabbit has a **car.** / **plane.**

2 Peppa and her family flew in
Miss Rabbit's / **Daddy Pig's** plane.

3 Peppa and George sat
in front of / **behind**
Mommy Pig and
Daddy Pig.

4 "That isn't a park. It's a
jungle!" / **mountain!"**
said Daddy Pig.

10 **Complete the sentences.
Write a—d.**

1 Pedro was on holiday .... c ....

2 The plane ....

3 "Hello, Pedro!" ....

4 "It's great in the jungle," ....

a flew down.

b said Pedro.

c in the jungle.

d said Peppa.

11 **Write the correct questions.**

1 (Was) (the) (fun) (jungle) (?)

Was the jungle fun?

2 (in) (Were) (jungle) (there)
(the) (puddles) (?)

....

....

3 (want) (Where) (Peppa) (to)
(go) (did) (?)

....

....

4 (Peppa) (with) (Who) (went) (?)

....

....

12 Do the crossword.

¹m	u	d	d	y

² p

³ p

⁴ p

Across

1 Peppa liked to jump in . . . puddles.

2 The jungle was fun, but there were no . . .

4 Peppa and her family enjoyed flying in a . . .

Down

1 Danny Dog loved the . . .

3 . . . Pony was on holiday in the jungle.

13 Circle the correct pictures.

1 Peppa heard **Bang! Clang! Bonk!** from this.

a

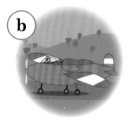
b

2 These went **Splosh! Squelch!**

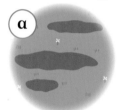
a

b

3 This hit the jungle floor with a **BUMP!**

a

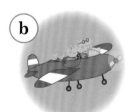
b

4 This said, "**Squeak!**"

a

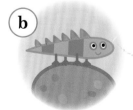
b

14 Circle the correct words.

1 The noise **Whhhiirrrrr!** came from

   a the mountain.   **b** the plane.

2 . . . loved the mountains.

   a Danny Dog   **b** Pedro Pony

3 Danny Dog was on the mountain with

   a Peppa Pig.   **b** Captain Dog.

4 Captain Dog said, "It's . . . here."

   a quite   **b** quiet

15 Circle the correct words.

1 The plane **fly** / **(flew)** to a desert.

2 Edmond and Emily Elephant **saw** / **sees** a lizard.

3 The lizard **run** / **ran** from them.

4 Suzy **want** / **wanted** to see Peppa.

5 Peppa **have** / **had** fun at the South Pole.

16 Ask and answer the questions with a friend. 💬

1 *Where did Peppa see Pedro and lots of animals?*

She saw them in the jungle.

2 Where were Danny and Captain Dog?

3 Where did Daddy Pig see a lizard?

4 Where did Peppa and her family see snow?

17 Order the story. Write 1—5.

_____ Miss Rabbit had a plane. "You can fly to the park," she said.

_____ Peppa and her family jumped in muddy puddles!

_____ Peppa and her family flew to a jungle, the mountains, a desert, and the South Pole.

__1__ Peppa wanted to go to the park, but the car stopped.

_____ "You can drive your car now," said Miss Rabbit.

Level 2

The Gingerbread Man
978-0-241-25442-4

Sly Fox and Red Hen
978-0-241-25443-1

The Monster Next Door
978-0-241-25444-8

Wild Animals
978-0-241-25445-5

Little Red Riding Hood
978-0-241-25446-2

Dinosaurs
978-0-241-25447-9

Topsy and Tim The Big Race
978-0-241-25448-6

Goes to the Treehouse
978-0-241-25449-3

Sports Day
978-0-241-26222-1

Going on a Picnic
978-0-241-26221-4

Peter Rabbit and the Angry Owl
978-0-241-28369-1

Superhero Max
978-0-241-28368-4

We Can Help!
978-0-241-28367-7

Daddy Pig's New Van
978-0-241-28371-4

School Trip
978-0-241-28372-1

The Peter Rabbit Club
978-0-241-29811-4

Daddy Pig's Office
978-0-241-29814-5

Spring is Here!
978-0-241-29809-1

Great Trains
978-0-241-29808-4

Hungry Animals
978-0-241-29844-2

Playing Football
978-0-241-31947-5

In a Plane
978-0-241-31945-1

Mountains
978-0-241-31948-2

Grimlock Stops the Decepticons
978-0-241-31954-3

Now you're ready for Level 3!